Ellen B. Jackson
The Bear in the Bathtub
illustrated by Margot Apple

Addison-Wesley

Text Copyright © 1981 by Ellen B. Jackson
Illustrations Copyright © 1981 by Margot Apple
All Rights Reserved
Addison-Wesley Publishing Company, Inc.
Reading, Massachusetts 01867
Printed in the United States of America

ABCDEFGHIJK-WZ-8987654321

Library of Congress Cataloging in Publication Data

Jackson, Ellen B
   The bear in the bathtub.

   SUMMARY: Andrew doesn't like to take baths, but when
a bear comes to stay in the bathtub, he sincerely
misses them.
   [1. Baths—Fiction. 2. Bears—Fiction] I. Apple,
Margot. II. Title.
PZ7.J13247Be   [E]   80-26535
ISBN 0-201-04701-2

To Ed
who knows about bears
EBJ

To Marshall Kofler
MA

Once there was a little boy who didn't like to take baths. Every night his mother would call, "Andrew come take your bath." And Andrew would yell back, "No! I don't like baths. I want to watch TV." But every night, rain or shine, Andrew's mother saw to it that Andrew took a bath.

One night Andrew's mother ran the warm water in the bathtub, opened the window just a crack to let the steam out, and went to call Andrew. Andrew sighed, turned off the TV set, and went into the bathroom.

His mother was washing dishes in the kitchen. When she turned around, there was Andrew standing in the doorway with a towel wrapped around him.

"Andrew, I thought I told you to take a bath," she said.

"I can't. There's a bear in the bathtub."

Andrew's mother sighed, "Well tell him to get out so you can take your bath."

Andrew went away, but a few minutes later he was back.

"He's still there."

Andrew's mother took Andrew by the hand and led him to the bathroom. Sure enough, there was a big brown bear in the bathtub.

"I think he got in through the window," said Andrew.

Andrew's mother said to the bear politely, "Mr. Bear, would you please leave the bathtub so my son Andrew can have his bath. It's getting quite late."

But the bear stayed in the bathtub.

Andrew's mother went to tell his father about the bear. Andrew's father scratched his head when he saw the big brown furry animal in the bathtub.

He said to the bear, "Mr. Bear, would you like something to eat? We have ice cream and cookies in the kitchen. You are welcome to have some if you will just come along and let my son Andrew take his bath."

But the bear stayed in the bathtub.

Andrew's mother pulled out the plug in the bathtub and said to Andrew, "I guess you can't take your bath tonight." And so for the first time ever, Andrew went to bed without his bath.

The next morning the bear was still in the bathtub. It was a school day, so Andrew's father drove Andrew to school. At recess the teacher called Andrew over and said, "Andrew, your face is dirty. Didn't you take a bath before school?"

Andrew said, "I couldn't. There's a bear in our bathtub."

The teacher didn't quite know what to say to that, so she just said, "Oh!"

After school Andrew raced home. The bear was still in the bathtub. There was a policeman in the bathroom trying to get him out while Andrew's mother and father watched.

"Now see here, Bear," said the policeman. "This will not do at all. I'm afraid I'll have to take you to jail if you don't leave this bathtub right now."

The bear just looked at the policeman.

The policeman grabbed the bear's leg and began to pull, but nothing happened. The bear was too heavy. Finally the policeman went away shaking his head.

Again that night Andrew went to bed without his bath.

The next day at school the other children didn't want to play with Andrew.

"You're so dirty," they said. "Why doesn't your mother give you a bath?"

"She can't," said Andrew, "because there's a bear in our bathtub."

"Bears don't live in bathtubs," said one very smart little girl. "They live in forests, and they eat fish and honey and all kinds of things, and they sleep all winter in caves."

"Not this one," said Andrew.

After school Andrew walked home slowly. He hoped the bear would be gone when he got there, but he knew there was still trouble when he saw the big red fire engines parked outside his house. The ladder from the hook-and-ladder truck was leaning against the bathroom window, and two firemen were standing on the top pulling at a rope that came from inside the house.

Andrew walked into the bathroom. Three more firemen had tied a rope around the bear's stomach and were pulling with all their might.

But the bear was still in the bathtub.

Once more Andrew had to go to bed without his bath.

The next day none of the children at school would talk to Andrew. When he tried to play with them, they would run away shouting, "You're too dirty. Go home and take a bath."

Andrew was sad, and he knew he had to think of a way to get the bear out of the bathtub.

When he got home from school his mother and father, the zoo keeper, and the mayor were standing in the bathroom. The mayor was talking to Andrew's mother and father.

He said, "We cannot have wild bears staying in bathtubs. If the bear will not leave, then we must tear down the bathtub and build a cage around the bear."

Andrew's mother looked worried.

"But we don't need a bear in the bathroom. We need a bathtub," she said.

"It must be done," said the mayor.

"Wait!" said Andrew. "I have an idea."

He went over to the bathtub and turned on the warm water. As the water was rising, he gave the bear a bar of soap and his special bottle of bubblebath. Then he went to his room and got his toy boats. He brought them back and put them in the water.

Then a strange thing happened. The bear began to splash around in the bathtub. He played with the toy boats, and then he soaped himself all over. Andrew scrubbed his back. Then the bear pulled the plug and climbed out of the bathtub. Andrew got a big towel and helped the bear dry himself off. Finally the bear gave Andrew a big bear hug and climbed out the bathroom window.

"Well, young man," said the mayor, "I see you know how to handle bears. If your mother and father will bring you down to the city hall, I'd like to give you the keys to the city for your quick thinking."

"That would be very nice, sir," said Andrew, "but first, if you don't mind, I'd like to take a bath."